EDGE BOOKS™

TRUE TALES OF SURVIVAL PRESENTS:

TRAPPED IN A CANYON!

ARON RALSTON'S STORY OF SURVIVAL

by Matt Doeden

Consultant:
Al Siebert, PhD
Author of *The Survivor Personality*

Capstone

Mankato, Minnesota

Edge Books are published by Capstone Press,
151 Good Counsel Drive, P.O. Box 669, Mankato, Minnesota 56002.
www.capstonepress.com

Library of Congress Cataloging-in-Publication Data
Doeden, Matt.
    Trapped in a canyon!: Aron Ralston's story of survival/by Matt Doeden.
    p. cm.—(Edge Books, true tales of survival)
    Includes bibliographical references and index.
    ISBN-13: 978-0-7368-6775-7 (hardcover)
    ISBN-10: 0-7368-6775-9(hardcover)
    ISBN-13: 978-0-7368-7865-4 (softcover pbk.)
    ISBN-10: 0-7368-7865-3 (softcover pbk.)
    1. Rock climbing accidents—Utah—Bluejohn Canyon—Juvenile literature. 2.
Ralston, Aron—Juvenile literature. 3. Desert survival—Utah—Bluejohn Canyon—
Juvenile literature. I. Title. II. Title: Aron Ralston's story of survival.
GV199.42.U8B48 2007
796.522'30289—dc22   2006032671

Summary: Describes how outdoorsman Aron Ralston survived six days with his
right arm trapped by a boulder in Canyonlands National Park and his eventual
self-amputation.

Editorial Credits
Mandy Robbins, editor; Jason Knudson, designer; Wanda Winch,
    photo researcher/photo editor

Photo Credits
AP/Wide World Photos/Ed Andrieski, 26–27; E Pablo Kosmicki, 28;
    Mickey Krakowski, 6–7
Aurora/Beth Wald, cover
Corbis/Scott T. Smith, 10–11; W. Perry Conway, 4–5
David Svilar, 22
Getty Images Inc./Aurora/Beth Wald, 12–13, 16–17, 21
iStockphoto Inc./Stephen Gibson, 24–25
Shutterstock/Alan Storey, 18–19 (background), 30–31 (background); Barry G. Hurt,
    back cover; Chris Hill, 1; Gennady Stetsenko, 21 (background); James M. Phelps, Jr.,
    14–15; Jim Lopes, 22–23 (background); Kevan O'Meara, 28–29 (background); Mike
    Donenfeld, 2–3; Pierdelune, 32 (background); Timothy Passmore, 18–19 (tool)
ZUMA Press/Photo by Aron Ralston, 8–9

1 2 3 4 5 6 12 11 10 09 08 07

TABLE of CONTENTS

CHAPTER 1

No Way Out

LEARN ABOUT:
- A DESPERATE SITUATION
- RUNNING OUT OF OPTIONS
- A DIFFICULT DECISION

Slot canyons, like the one Aron was trapped in, are like deep mazes in the ground.

Worst of all, Aron had failed to tell anyone of his plans.

Alone in the Utah desert, Aron Ralston was trapped. His right forearm was pinned between a huge boulder and a wall of Blue John Canyon.

As he fought off pain and panic, the 27-year-old outdoorsman knew that his situation was bleak. No blood was flowing into his trapped hand. He had a single bottle of water and just a bit of food. His only tool was a pocket knife multi-tool. He had nothing to protect him from the chilly night air.

Worst of all, Aron had failed to tell anyone of his plans. Days passed before anyone even noticed he was missing. Even when his boss, friends, and family did notice, they had no idea where to look for him.

5

For five desperate days, Aron tried to free himself. He chipped away at the large rock with his multi-tool. He tried to move the 800 pound (360 kilogram) boulder, but it wouldn't budge. Nothing helped. Aron had little hope of rescue and only enough supplies for a day's hike. Tired, hungry, and thirsty, Aron knew he wouldn't last much longer.

As the sun set on the Utah desert, Aron had a grim realization. There was only one way to free himself. He had to cut off his arm.

EDGE FACT

Aron wrote a book about his ordeal called *Between a Rock and a Hard Place*. It was published in 2004.

Aron started his hike at Horseshoe Canyon Trailhead.

CHAPTER 2

A SIMPLE HIKE

Aron had climbed 45 of Colorado's highest peaks before his hike into Blue John Canyon.

LEARN ABOUT:
- A TRUE OUTDOORSMAN
- INTO BLUE JOHN CANYON
- TRAPPED IN AN INSTANT

Aron had always enjoyed the outdoors. Living in Aspen, Colorado, Aron worked in a store called Ute Mountaineering, which sold climbing gear. He spent his free time climbing mountains, using ropes to rappel down cliffs, hiking, and biking. One of his goals was to climb all 59 of Colorado's mountains with peaks of at least 14,000 feet (4,300 meters). And if that wasn't challenge enough, he planned to climb them all during winter months. By 2003, Aron had completed 45 of the climbs.

Compared to his other adventures, the one-day bike ride and hike on Saturday, April 26, seemed simple. He didn't tell his friends or family where he would be. He just packed a day's supplies and took off.

INTO THE CANYON

After a 15-mile (24 kilometers) bike ride, Aron began his hike into a remote area of Blue John Canyon. Early on, he was surprised to meet two other hikers. He introduced himself and walked with the two women. They asked him to join them on their route, but Aron was determined to hike to a spot called the Great Gallery. There, he could see ancient stone paintings called petroglyphs.

Alone, Aron squeezed through the canyon's tight spaces. The sun was hot above him, but the shaded canyon was cool. He kept a close eye on the sky, knowing the danger of being in a slot canyon during a storm. Even a little rainfall could cause a flash flood in such a spot.

The petroglyphs in the Great Gallery
are between 3,000 and 4,000 years old.

11

Blue John Canyon was named for outlaw John Griffith, nicknamed "Blue John." Legend says he kept stolen horses in the area during the late 1800s.

After about 40 minutes, Aron came upon several chockstones. These fallen boulders were wedged between the canyon walls. He climbed over a few of these stones and crawled underneath others. Aron was moving quickly, but not rushing. He was just enjoying being alone with nature and listening to the music pumping through his headphones.

12

This 800-pound (360-kilogram) boulder fell on Aron's arm, crushing his hand.

A LOOSE BOULDER

Aron came upon yet another large chockstone. He stepped gently onto it, making sure it was stable. He began to lower himself over the other side. But as he moved, the stone started to shift. Worried the stone might fall, Aron let go of it. He fell to the canyon floor below.

The boulder, now freed, fell toward him. Instinctively, Aron threw up his hands to protect his head. With a crash, the heavy stone smashed into his left arm and rolled off. When it came to rest, The chockstone had pinned Aron's right arm tightly against the wall.

13

A wave of pain and panic came over Aron. He hurled himself against the fallen boulder, desperate to move it and pull his arm free. He threw every bit of strength he had at the immense rock, but it was no use. His arm was stuck.

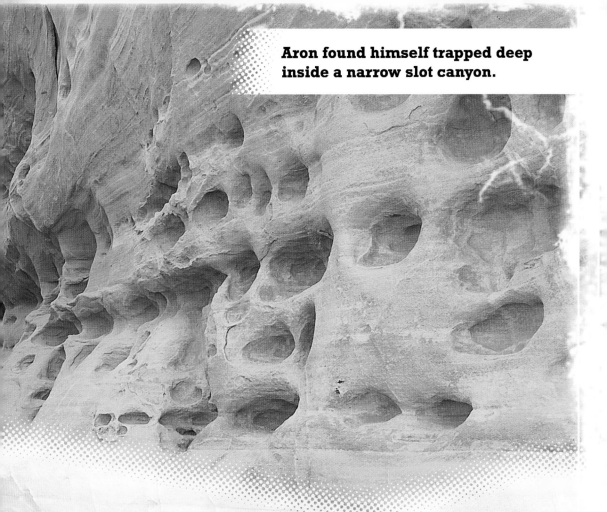

Aron found himself trapped deep inside a narrow slot canyon.

Aron forced himself to remain calm. He took stock of his supplies. He had two bean burritos and only 20 ounces (.6 liters) of water. Aron allowed himself a sip of water every 90 minutes. He used his multi-tool to cut apart his backpack for shelter from the night air. The situation seemed hopeless, but Aron did everything he could to survive.

041326

CHAPTER 3

LAST RESORT

LEARN ABOUT:
- DIFFICULT DAYS
- LOSING HOPE
- ONE LAST ATTEMPT

While Aron was trapped, sunlight reached him less than one hour per day.

> ## On Tuesday, Aron swallowed his last sip of water.

Aron kept chipping away at the boulder. He looked for a weakness in the rock but couldn't find one. Hours of chipping became days, and Aron was barely making any progress.

A FAILED ATTEMPT

On Tuesday, Aron swallowed his last sip of water. By this time, he knew his friends would wonder why they hadn't seen him. But they still had no idea where he was. Now, without any water, Aron couldn't afford to wait any longer. It was time to try his most desperate solution. He took out his multi-tool.

This tool is similar to the tool that Aron used to try to chip away at the boulder.

EDGE FACT

In one of Aron's good-bye messages to friends and family, he said, "Bring love and peace and happiness and beautiful lives into the world in my honor."

Days of chipping at the boulder had left the main blade dull. But Aron still tried to cut himself free. As Aron began sawing his arm, he noticed that the dull blade barely broke the skin. It would never saw through hard bone. He gave up.

Although Aron didn't know it, by Thursday, May 1, a full rescue effort was underway. Park rangers had found his truck, but since he'd biked to Blue John Canyon, they couldn't find him.

Meanwhile, Aron was desperate. He'd been without water for two days and knew he wouldn't survive another night. On a video camera he'd brought in his backpack, he taped his goodbyes to his friends and family. He carved his name and the letters "RIP" in the canyon walls. The letters are often seen on grave stones. They stand for "rest in peace."

Aron was prepared to die.

19

BREAKING FREE

Aron's body was shutting down. Lack of food and water and the cold night air were taking their toll. He had one last, desperate idea. He twisted his body and applied as much force to his trapped arm as he could.

Pop! One of the bones in his forearm snapped. Pop! The other one snapped, in nearly the same spot as the first. With both bones snapped, he wouldn't have to cut through them. For the first time, Aron had hope. He tied a tourniquet around his arm to stop the bleeding and took out his dull blade.

The amputation was slow and painful. Using the two blades in his multi-tool, Aron cut through his arm one layer at a time. He sliced through skin, muscle, and tendon. But the worst part was cutting through the nerve. The pain felt like flames shooting up his entire arm.

After about an hour, Aron fell backward onto the canyon floor. He'd freed himself, minus his right hand, from the canyon wall.

The surgery Aron performed on his arm left streaks of blood along the canyon wall.

This hiker is standing at the top of the cliff that Aron managed to rappel down with one arm.

A LONG HIKE

Aron couldn't go back the way he'd come. He had gone down several sharp drop-offs and could never climb back up. He had to finish the route he'd planned almost a week before. With his arm spurting blood, he stumbled through the canyon. Finally, Aron reached the point in the hike he'd been dreading. He had to rappel down a 60-foot (18 meters) cliff before he could hike back to the road.

Amazingly, Aron managed to set up his ropes and lower himself safely down the cliff. At the bottom, he found a pool of standing water and guzzled it. Then he began hiking again in the hot desert sun. But by this time, Aron had lost about 25 percent of his blood. His body was slowly going into shock. With 7 miles (11 kilometers) to go, it seemed like he still wouldn't make it out of Blue John Canyon alive.

But Aron kept going. Soon, he saw three other hikers. A Dutch couple and their son had come out to see the canyon. Aron called to them for help. The family gave him what little food and water they had. The mother and son went for help, and the father stayed to help Aron walk.

Aron walked 6 miles (10 kilometers) before he was picked up by a rescue helicopter.

Before the woman reached help, a rescue helicopter spotted Aron. The rescue workers rushed out to help the injured and weary hiker. Against all odds, Aron Ralston was going to survive.

25

CHAPTER 4

SURVIVOR

LEARN ABOUT:

- **RESCUE AND RELIEF**
- **BECOMING BIG NEWS**
- **FULL SPEED AHEAD**

The helicopter rushed Aron to a hospital, where doctors removed more of his infected arm. His parents, thrilled to learn that their son was alive, hurried to his side. Aron's father was still trying to get back from a business trip. But when Aron woke up, he and his mother enjoyed a tearful reunion.

Though Aron's parents were upset about his injury, they were simply happy to have their son alive.

The loss of his right arm hasn't
slowed Aron Ralston down a bit.

INSTANT CELEBRITY

Aron's ordeal was front-page news around the world. He appeared on *Late Night with David Letterman* and was named one of *GQ* magazine's Men of the Year. He gave speeches about his experience all over the United States.

Aron's taste for adventure hasn't faded since his brush with death. He now has an artificial arm with specialized attachments. One device is a pick that he can use while climbing. Aron has continued his plan to climb all of Colorado's peaks. He still hikes, rides his bike, and rappels down cliffs.

Adventurers often use the word "epic" to describe life-and-death struggles between man and nature. Aron says that he wouldn't trade his epic for anything. His story has inspired millions of people and helped make him the survivor that he is today.

GLOSSARY

amputate (AM-pyuh-tate)—to cut off someone's arm, leg, or other body part, usually because the part is damaged

canyon (KAN-yuhn)—a deep, narrow valley

chockstone (CHOK-stone)—a boulder that has become wedged between two canyon walls

nerve (NURV)—a thin fiber that carries messages of feeling from the body to the brain

petroglyph (PEH-trah-glif)—a picture or word carved on a rock

rappel (ruh-PEL)—to slide down a strong rope

tendon (TEN-duhn)—a band of tissue that connects a muscle to a bone

tourniquet (TUR-nuh-ket)—a tight wrapping made to prevent a major loss of blood from a wound

READ MORE

Nadeau, Isaac. *Canyons.* Library of Landforms. New York: PowerKids Press, 2006.

Ralston, Aron. *Between a Rock and a Hard Place.* New York: Atria Books, 2004.

Riley, Peter D. *Survivor's Science in the Desert.* Survivor's Science. Chicago: Raintree, 2005.

INTERNET SITES

FactHound offers a safe, fun way to find Internet sites related to this book. All of the sites on FactHound have been researched by our staff.

Here's how:

1. Visit *www.facthound.com*

2. Choose your grade level.

3. Type in this book ID **0736867759** for age-appropriate sites. You may also browse subjects by clicking on letters, or by clicking on pictures and words.

4. Click on the **Fetch It** button.

FactHound will fetch the best sites for you!

INDEX